Wakefield Libraries
& Information Services

This book should be returned by the last date stamped above. You may renew the loan personally, by post or telephone for a further period if the book is not required by another reader.

First published 2003 by
A & C Black Publishers Ltd
37 Soho Square, London, W1D 3QZ

www.acblack.com

Text copyright © 2003 Lynda Waterhouse
Illustrations copyright © 2003 Martin Remphry

ISBN 0-7136-6285-9

A CIP catalogue for this book is available from the British Library.

A&C Black uses paper produced with elemental chlorine-free
pulp, harvested from managed sustained forests.

Printed and bound in Spain by G. Z. Printek, Bilbao.

LYNDA WATERHOUSE

Drucilla and the Cracked Pot

Illustrated by
Martin Remphry

A & C Black • London

To David Harris

Chapter One

I'm Drucilla and I've got this terrible reputation for causing trouble. It's not my fault that things happen when I'm around. Nine times out of ten my little brother, Marcus, has something to do with it. Does he ever get the blame? Oh no, he just puts on this 'I am only a seven-year-old boy' routine and gets away with blue murder.

I was born in Rome but I don't remember much about it. We came to Britain when I was three. It's a wild place with terrible weather and rough barbarians but I like it here. Grampus is always banging on about Rome. He misses the sunshine, the food and cheering on The Blues – his favourite chariot team at the Coliseum. Mum never mentions the 'R' word but she's usually too busy making pots to say much about anything. My dad got himself killed fighting the Gauls so ever since, we've had to earn our own keep.

I love living in Londinium! Ships arrive from all over the Empire bringing all sorts of weird and wonderful things, from exotic sauces to elephants! Villas and luxury development apartments are springing up everywhere for all the rich retired soldiers. Everyone's far too busy to care what a ten-year-old kid is up to. You can get away with all sorts if you are careful and move fast.

To try to keep me out of trouble Mum gives me lots of errands to do. That day, she had sent me to the baker's for some honey cakes. As I was walking back the long way via the riverbank a brown scruffy dog barked at me and a voice called out, 'Hi there, Drucilla!'

It was Horace the Offal and his dog, Cano. Horace collects the insides of animals and boils them up for glue. In his spare time he sifts through people's rubbish. Horace held up five fingers to me and gave me one of his toothless grins.

'No way!' I yelled back so loudly that I nearly choked on a piece of honey cake (I had to test if they were stale or not).

Horace giggled and Cano barked at me again as his tail tried to wag itself from his body.

I held up three fingers back to them.

Horace giggled again.

When he heard about the torture that Mum puts me through every evening with her nit comb and earwax spoon, Horace had suggested we make a bit of a competition out of it. The aim is to see who could collect the most bugs each week. To give me a chance, it's between Cano and me. There would be no contest against Horace. He is the grubbiest person in the whole of Londinium. Imagine the stink of a barrel of rotting fish, times it by ten, mix with two rotten eggs and a sweaty sock and you've almost got Horace on a good day. If you don't stay downwind of him, you're dead meat.

I was about to offer him one of my cakes when a reedy soothsayer's voice piped up behind me, 'Beware the too sweet tooth for it will turn to bad!'

Before I could say 'Sybil' she'd snatched two cakes and stuffed them into her mouth. Her cheeks bulged as her one tooth worked to chew on the cake.

Sybil did her 'seeing into the future' training

at a very famous oracle in Greece. She earns a living by reading the future in the animal entrails that Horace collects. Once, when I asked her if Mum, Grampus, Marcus and I would ever make it back to Rome she had replied, 'One day people will travel across the sky in the belly of a large iron bird, so anything is possible.'

That's the trouble with Sybil – her readings are a teeny bit out. Not by much, just the odd thousand years.

She swallowed down the last bit of cake and continued.

'In years to come no one will read the future in animal entrails. Instead they will be flattened, cooked and eaten between bread and red sugar sauce. All over the Empire, identical shops will spring up to sell the flattened meat. Children will beg their mothers to feed it to them. Their bellies will grow so fat that their tunics will have to be made from expanding material.'

Sybil waved her bony fingers in the air as she spoke. Horace and I followed their movement through the air until my eyes crossed.

I mumbled, 'Phew, I'm glad I don't live in this future where everyone goes crazy for animal tubes.'

Sybil smiled and said, 'Burgers!'

'There's no need to be rude, I was only saying,' I snapped back.

Sybil smiled again. 'These animal tubes will be called "burgers". Now, Drucilla, dear one, do try and stay out of mischief's way today.'

If she'd been able to see into the near future she'd have known it was going to be one of the worst days of my life.

Chapter Two

Lucky for me, Mum had been too wrapped up in making an order of pots to notice how long I'd been. Grampus had taken Marcus off to the baths for some male bonding and grime-scraping-off, so he couldn't give me one of his famous 'in my day' lectures.

Mum looked hot and flustered so I decided to make myself useful for once. Mum works incredibly hard. Grampus says that in Rome she had been a rich lady, famed for her beauty and charm. He was really proud when his son wanted to marry her. Mum used to spend all day lying on a couch eating grapes but gave it all up to marry Dad. Now she spends all day mixing clay and loading it into a baking kiln.

Grampus often says, 'One day her family will come to take her back.'

Mum shakes her head and replies, 'When Hades freezes over.'

I was scratching some numbers into a wax tablet and trying to make them add up when the door opened and in marched a large officer of the Roman army. He must have just arrived from Rome because he wasn't splattered in Londinium grime or rusted over from being endlessly rained on.

'By Jupiter!' He banged his fist so hard on the counter that my teeth rattled and I longed to bite into his stubby fingers. Bang! His fist went down again.'Do you know who I am?'

I scanned his face – the square jaw, cruel blue eyes, wobbly lip and big teeth.

'Do you know who I am?' he repeated.

A big, fat donkey sprang immediately to my mind.

Before I could reply he placed a bowl on the counter and said in an angry voice, 'I, Pontius Maximus, will not stand for this incompetence! There is a crack in this pot!'

I gave him my best Queen-Boudicca-about-to-slaughter-the-Roman-army look. I imagined myself as the Queen of the Britons prodding him with my spear.

Mum inspected the bowl and said, 'I can assure you, the bowl was in mint condition when it left the shop. The rest of your dinner service will also be perfect.'

Pontius Maximus lifted his big Roman nose in the air and sniffed.

'It had better be. I have to entertain some very important guests. I had heard that this was the finest pottery in Londinium. Obviously standards are terribly low here. I will call back in two days to check on the progress.'

As he turned to go, I treated his back to my horrendous bug-eyed-demon-ascending-from-the-swamp face. It's so grotesque that it makes Marcus physically sick.

He turned back again and I had to fake an instant coughing fit.

'There will be no payment until I am completely satisfied.' He stuck his chin out from under his helmet and puffed out his chest like an overgrown pigeon, before turning back round towards the door. 'Nothing less than perfection will do.' He sniffed again.

Just as he was reaching the door his foot landed smack bang in the middle of Marcus's toy chariot. It propelled him through the door and into the street where he spun round three times before crashing to the ground, revealing what officers in the Roman army are wearing underneath their tunics at the moment: bright purple underpants with golden eagles printed on them.

Pontius Maximus's face turned a matching purple and he glared at me, saying, 'What are you staring at, girl?'

Before I could reply 'You, you fat lummox', Mum elbowed me out of the way and began dazzling him with one of her super charmer smiles as a small crowd began to gather.

She whispered, 'I'll give you a good discount on the dinner service. Please come back.'

'Need any help here?'

A familiar toothless grin loomed over us. What on Earth were Horace and Sybil doing here?

Everybody took three steps backwards.

Pontius lifted his head and took a deep breath as if he were about to bark an order. As his nostrils filled with the famous 'Horace stink' his face went from purple to green and twitched like someone had jabbed him in the bottom with a red-hot poker. When he recovered, he kicked Horace roughly out of the way.

Cano growled as Sybil's voice piped up, 'Lo! The Roman army brought to its knees. It is a sign, an omen.'

Sybil was building herself up for a full-scale rant. When she gets really wound up she tears at her hair and rolls around on the floor.

When she saw me she stopped, mid-rant, and said, 'Oh, Drucilla, there you are, dear! Horace and I were coming to find you. You dropped this.'

She handed me a coin. The change from the honey cakes! I'd have been in big trouble if I'd lost that.

Pontius had got halfway up and was pausing for breath when Cano chose that moment to sink his teeth into the purple and gold underpants. No one hurts Horace without Cano doing something about it.

I grabbed a bucket of water from the tanner's shop and threw it over Pontius and Cano to unlock his jaws.

Did I get any thanks for it? All I got was glared at like I'd done something wrong.

Chapter Three

When Marcus came back from the baths and found out what had happened, he howled, 'He broke my chariot and I never even got to see him slide across the shop and land on his bottom.'

Typical reaction! It wouldn't even occur to him to apologise for leaving his toys lying around.

Grampus was cross too. He kept shaking his head and muttering, 'Purple underpants indeed! In my day we didn't wear anything – not even in the snow.'

Mum looked up from the hearth where she was stirring the cooking pot. 'Do we really need to know that, Father?'

'I bet he cracked the pot himself. Looked at his reflection in the glaze,' I muttered.

Marcus changed from howling to shrieking. 'He's a crackpot! He's a crackpot! And he broke my chariot and didn't offer to pay.'

Mum sighed. 'He's a rich customer and I need the money to pay the rent. Besides, he is an officer of the Roman army, like your father.'

I cut in, 'Dad would never have been so rude, not even to a slave.'

'Not even to the dog of a slave,' Marcus added.

'Not even to a flea on the dog of a slave.' Grampus shook his fist.

Mum smiled. 'At least we've got each other and—'

On cue we all chanted, 'People will always need pots!'

It was our family's rallying cry. We always shouted it when one of us got upset or there wasn't enough money for the rent.

The door of the shop opened and my best friend, Philip, came in, carrying a small leather bag.

Grampus jumped up and rubbed his hands with glee. 'Aha, my new purge!'

Grampus believes that swallowing herbs that turn your insides to fast-flowing volcanic lava can solve all the problems in the world. He's always saying, 'If only Julius Caesar had taken a few more purges then he would have known better than to trust that Brutus fellow.'

Philip's father used to be a slave to a rich man. That was until his master ate some off figs that his wife had prepared specially. Philip's dad cured him and was granted his freedom. When they have saved enough money they plan to go back to Greece. Londinium is full of people from all over the Empire. Some are here to make their fortunes and some are here to spend all their money.

As Philip handed over the pouch he warned, 'Dad says to be careful, it's a very strong laxative. Only a tiny pinch of the herbs in a drink is enough to do the trick.'

I stood in front of the cooking fire. 'Keep that bag away from the stew pot!'

Mum ignored me and smiled at Philip. 'Stay and eat with us,' she said. She thinks he is 'a sensible boy'.

Philip shook his head. 'I have to go and collect some plants by the river. Early evening is the best time for gathering them.'

'Can I help Philip, Mum?' I asked. Hanging about the river with Philip is great fun. It would also mean getting out of the washing-up and hearth-sweeping.

Mum thought it over for an agonisingly long time before saying, 'All right, but eat something first, don't be too late back – and take your brother with you.'

'Ah, Mum! Remember what happened last time?' I protested.

Marcus stuck his bottom lip out. 'It wasn't my fault. Anyone can slip on a fish.'

'In the middle of a field? I don't think so.' I stamped my foot. Marcus was always ruining my life with his presence.

Mum gave me one of her 'you're-pushing-your-luck' faces and so I kept my mouth shut and let Marcus come along with us.

As we walked along, I noticed how the sunset turned Philip's golden hair to something more like my red colour. I liked to imagine that he was my brother instead of you-know-who.

'A man came into the surgery today,' Philip began as he untied the small collecting sack from around his waist. 'He was really upset, wouldn't stop crying and shaking. It took Dad ages to calm him down.'

'What was the matter? Did he have the plague?' Marcus's eyes widened.

'No, worse than that. He thought he was a pair of drapes, so Dad told him to pull himself together.'

Philip's face stayed straight, apart from a faint flicker about the lips. I half groaned and half laughed.

Marcus frowned and said, 'I once spent a day thinking I was a cushion. I had to lie down on the couch all day and do nothing. I changed back when Mum said she was going to hang me out in the yard and beat the dust out of me with a big stick. I don't think I'd like being drapes.

I'm off to look for fish.'

He picked up the sack and disappeared down a bank, leaving Philip and me looking at each other blankly. We can't work out if Marcus is barking mad or a genius.

After we'd rummaged around the river's edge for the right plants, Philip and I scrambled up the stony bank side and sat on a large tree stump beneath a huge oak tree. Marcus wandered further up the bank, muttering something about finding a fish.

Philip sighed. 'This whole area used to be full of trees.'

I nodded toward a newly-built warehouse. 'They're still here, only they've been turned into buildings.'

On the north side, a couple of large ships were moored and beyond them was the newly-built Forum. Behind that were the two hills that marked the boundaries of Londinium.

Philip pointed to the larger of the two ships. 'Just come in from Rome. By all accounts it's brought some impressive visitors.'

'I've had a bellyfull of so-called impressive people,' I groaned and told him about Pontius Maximus and the way he had treated us today.

'So, you see, I'd much rather spend time with ordinary people like Horace and Sybil. They accept you for what you are.' I sighed and flopped down on my back in the long grass.

'Horace came to see my dad once …' Philip began.

I sighed. 'This isn't one of your corny jokes, is it, because I can only stand one of those a day.'

'No, this is for real. He came to see my dad because he was worried that Cano smelt and Dad didn't want his feelings hurt. Dad gave him some special dog soap. He told him to use it first so that Cano would know it was safe. Only trouble was that after Horace had used it, Cano ran off – he couldn't smell his master anymore. It took three weeks and a lot of rubbish-sifting before Cano came back to Horace.'

I pulled up a handful of grass and said, 'I hate it when people try to change you!'

Philip jabbed me in the ribs. 'Roman soldier heading this way at full speed and looking like he's going to attack a whole tribe of barbarians single-handedly.'

We ducked down behind the tree as the soldier approached. As I glanced up and saw his face, my stomach purged itself and dropped down into my feet. It was Pontius Maximus looking as mad as Hades and heading towards us!

Chapter Four

He stomped past the tree, crushing flowers with his big leather sandals. He charged down towards the riverbank, muttering something like, 'Let me be rid of them!'

He was definitely up to no good. We crawled down the riverbank after him on our bellies. On the way down I scraped my knee on the sharp end of a stone. As I turned to rub my knee my hair got tangled up in a hawthorn bush. Ducking down to avoid being scratched, I dunked half my face and hair in a smelly muddy puddle. When we reached the ridge there was no sign of Pontius and every bit of me was hurting or covered in stinking mud.

'Let me go. If he recognises you he may cancel the order,' Philip whispered.

'I don't think my own mother would recognise me now,' I snapped back, trying to wipe some of the mud off my face. Still, best not take any chances – Pontius didn't look too pleased the last time I saw him when I 'rescued' him from Cano.

Just then we heard a mighty roar of 'Go away, you useless abomination!' followed by a large splash. Then we saw Pontius's helmet bobbing up and down as it disappeared down a track along the riverbank.

It was then that I remembered about Marcus. 'He's hurled Marcus in!'

I jumped to my feet and charged down the ridge. Marcus was bound to have got in Pontius's way and got himself thrown in. I felt like doing it myself often enough. If Marcus had gone and got himself drowned then Mum would never forgive me!

I tore down the muddy bank faster than the gods' messenger, Mercury, on a mission. Halfway down I saw Marcus and began waving my arms in relief whilst fighting off a strange urge to hug him.

When Marcus saw me, he froze in his tracks,

then let out this strange scream and turned to run. It was like he'd seen a monster or something.

'Marcus!' Philip shouted. 'It's us.'

Marcus stopped. He looked at me out of the corner of his eye for a long time before saying, 'You look weird and you've lost a sandal.'

'It must have come off when I was racing down the hill to save your life. What happened when Pontius saw you?'

Ungrateful wretch!

Marcus stuck his bottom lip out. 'That soldier was Pontius? I wish I'd known because he owes me money for breaking my toy. I was down by the reeds looking for fish when I heard shouting. He threw something that splashed near me. When he'd gone I fished it out.' He held out a bit of metal. 'Do you think it's worth anything?'

'It's probably a bit of his armour that's broken off. He's so bad-tempered, something like that would be enough to send him into a rage,' I replied.

'It's got writing on one side.' Marcus turned it over. 'I wonder what it says?'

Philip came up behind us and said softly, 'It's a curse.'

I tried to snatch it from Marcus. 'Throw it back – quick!'

Marcus stuffed it up his tunic. 'No, it's my curse and I want to keep it.'

I looked at Philip. He has a brain the size of the Empire. He would know what to do.

Philip wrinkled his brow. 'Pontius has written his terrible curse down on this offering, and thrown it into the river for the gods. The gods don't like people interfering in their business. As we have intercepted the curse, we have to deal with it.'

Marcus's eyes popped. 'So, if he hates someone, we have to hate them too? I'm quite good at being mean to people.'

A terrible thought hit me like a thunderbolt! 'What if he's cursed Mum for the cracked pot? Philip, read what it says.'

Reluctantly, Marcus handed over the curse.

Philip screwed up his eyes. 'It's very scratchy and I'm not as good at reading Latin as I am Greek.'

'Sybil! She's an expert on these matters. Let's take it to her,' I suggested.

'It's too late to go now. We'd better deal with this first thing in the morning,' Philip replied.

So we put the curse in the collecting bag and stuffed it down Marcus's tunic. It took us ages to find my sandal, which was buried in a pile of mud. One of the straps had broken so I had to tie the snapped ends into a knot. It meant that I had to hold my foot still and lift my leg high to keep it in place as I walked.

Philip and Marcus found my funny flip-flap walk hilarious. All I wanted to do was go home, have a wash and crawl upstairs to bed. Underneath the mud I was covered in scratches and scrapes.

We said goodbye to Philip on the corner and carried on home.

There was a customer in the shop. Mum usually closes the shop section early so we can have some family time together before bed.

I grabbed Marcus's arm and hissed through

clenched teeth, 'Not a word about Pontius and the curse.'

Even through the lamplight I could see that Mum had a strained smile on her face. Grampus was nervously hopping about the shop and tugging at the few scraps of hair he had left. The customer was a tall, round woman, draped in a long red cloak and a flowing dress. The jewels in her ears sparkled.

She was inspecting Mum's hands and shaking her head.

'Your hands used to be so soft before you married into that family!' She gave Grampus a disapproving look.

When Mum saw us she said in a strange voice, 'Ah, children, there you are. We have a surprise visitor from Rome – my sister, your Aunt Livia.'

The large woman turned round. I stepped out from the shadow. She looked at Marcus first and smiled and then I took a 'flip-flap' step towards her.

Her eyes filled with horror as she gasped and then slumped across the counter in a dead faint.

What had I done?

Chapter Five

Early the next morning, Grampus splashed a jug of cold water over my face. 'You remind me of those Barbarians that Hadrian had such trouble with on the Borders. All wild hair, face paint and gnashing teeth.'

Mum scraped my face with a rough cloth. 'How could you let yourself get into such a state?'

'It's just mud and scratches. I don't know what the fuss is about,' I grumbled.

In the next bed, Marcus was still snoring. He could sleep through an earthquake.

Mum set about me with a comb. 'No wonder Livia fainted at the sight of you. You look like you've been dragged through a hedge backwards and your legs are all splattered in mud. What were you up to?'

There was no way I could tell her that, so I sat up and asked, 'Who is this Aunt Livia? You've never mentioned her before.'

'There's not much to tell. She's just arrived from Rome and she's coming round again this afternoon. So we are going to make a better impression today, aren't we?' She tugged hard on my hair.

'Don't see why we have to put on airs and graces for your sister!' Grampus muttered.

'I just don't want Livia thinking badly of us all,' Mum snapped back.

'How far would those fancy ways get her without the might of the Roman army behind her? I'm proud of my son. We'd all be cursed without the army.'

I jumped out of bed when I heard the word 'curse'.

'Shall I go and get some fresh bread and cakes?' I asked.

Mum eyed me suspiciously.

I stared back at her. 'What? I'm only trying to be nice. What's wrong with that?'

Mum shook her head as she gave me some coins. 'I'm not sure, Drucilla, but I bet there is something.'

'I'll take Marcus with me to give you some peace,' I added and Mum jumped up.

'*Now* I'm sure you're up to something. Make sure you're back within the hour while Grampus and I try to get on with Pontius's plates.'

I reached for the jug of cold water and leaned over Marcus's bed.

* * *

Five minutes later, Marcus and I stepped outside. There was a slight breeze and a damp drizzle in the air. Even though it was morning, the street was full of people. Next to our shop was a tanner, a locksmith, a glassmaker and a sandal repair shop. There was always noise and people. We knocked on Philip's door. It opened slowly.

Philip held his fingers to his lips and joined us outside. He whispered, 'Dad's last customer is a bit upset. Dad told him to take two spoonfuls of cat's milk every day. The man looked very worried and asked, "Doctor, how can I get milk from a cat?" My dad shook his head and said, "All you do is distract it and then take the saucer away!"'

I punched Philip in the arm. 'Watch out, because one day, I will hurl a curse in the river that says something about you and bad doctor jokes.'

We made our way through the narrow alleyways that led to Sybil's place. Outside, Marcus caused a minor panic when he couldn't find the curse. It turned up in his back tunic pocket.

There was a piece of material instead of a door to Sybil's home. We stood there, hesitating, until Marcus piped up, 'Knock, knock.'

'Who's there?' a voice asked.

Philip, who was standing behind me and

couldn't hear properly, said, 'Who?'

I replied, 'Who "who"?'

'Sorry, I don't speak to owls!' Sybil shouted through the cloth. 'Anyone else can come in.'

There was a series of bells above the door frame that jangled when you pushed through. As Sybil spent most of her time looking into the future, she had no time for the present and tidying up. Every available space was filled with scraps of cloth, old beads or bits of bone. Sybil cleared a bench so that we could sit down.

'Is this about that soldier?' she asked, drawing a bit of woollen rag around her shoulders.

We all nodded.

'Got a funny feeling in my waters about him.'

I explained about Pontius and what had happened by the river.

Marcus took out the piece of metal. 'I've got the curse here …'

Philip added, 'We were wondering if you could let us know what it is all about.'

Sybil took hold of the curse and held it close to her chest for a long time with her eyes closed.

'When is she going to read the writing?' Marcus whispered to me.

I kicked his leg and said, 'Shh.'

Sybil then wandered around the room, holding the curse above her head, swaying and humming.

Marcus kicked me back and hissed, 'I don't know much about reading but most people need their eyes open to do it.'

Even Philip was looking worried. So I spoke out, 'We need to be getting back home, Sybil. Could you tell us about the words on the curse?'

Sybil froze in the middle of the room. She made a squeaking noise and jumped up saying, 'Words, words, words. One day words will come too easily. People will tap them on to letter boards and into boxes. Words will race through the air faster than a racing chariot. What will these words say? Earth-shattering news and information will be passed, but mainly it will be

35

jokes and nonsense. Messages in text that mean nothing.'

Marcus stood up and bellowed, 'Sybil, can you read?'

She clicked back into normal mode, smiled and said, 'I can read messages in the insides of animals and the patterns that flights of birds make in the sky.'

'Can you read symbols scratched on wax, in tablets of stone or on papyrus?' Philip asked.

'Oh, no, can't do that. Not really in a soothsayer's line of business.' Sybil smiled at us.

We all stood up to leave. Marcus snatched up the curse, muttering under his breath.

As we reached the door, Horace poked his head through the curtain. 'Thought I heard voices. Is everything all right? Can I help?'

We all took three steps backwards.

'Only if you can read,' grumbled Marcus.

I quickly added, 'Words, not animal entrails. We need someone to decipher this.'

Horace picked up the piece of metal and scratched his head. (Everyone except me took another two steps back.) Finally he said, 'I'll need my eye-enhancers but I think I can do it.'

Sybil reached this glass contraption down from a shelf and Horace wrapped the eye-enhancers round his face. The thick glass made his eyeballs look ten times bigger.

He carefully looked at the curse again, shook his head, muttered a few words under his breath and then burst out laughing.

'Well! Strike me down with Vulcan's hammer—'

Grampus burst into the room looking like he'd been hit where it hurts by Vulcan's great hammer.

'Come along with me now. The mood your mother is in, if you don't hurry up we'll all wish we were in Hades!'

I just had time to see Philip slip the curse into his collecting bag.

Chapter Six

Grampus whisked Marcus and me out of the door and marched us up the street muttering, 'Livia has turned up early with some harebrained scheme to take you and your mother to a beauty parlour.' His cloak flapped against his bony knees. 'She says you're not presentable.'

I shook my head. 'I've heard they do terrible things to you in those places.'

Grampus looked at me. 'They arrange your hair and clean your face. Sounds like real torture to me.'

'I want to go!' Marcus whined.

'You can come to the Temple of Mithras with me.' Grampus patted his head.

'All you do is sit around drinking wine and playing boring cards,' Marcus replied.

'We are involved in a mysterious rite!' Grampus snapped back.

I continued, 'At least they don't poke you and twist you about. At the beauty parlour, they pull hairs out of your eyebrows one at a time and then they bake you in hot mud!'

'I thought you liked mud,' Marcus said.

'Doesn't it cost a lot of money to go there?' I asked, ignoring Marcus.

'Livia is paying. Always did have more money than sense. In my day, we didn't have much money. Sometimes the army would pay us in salt instead.' Grampus shook his head.

'Salt!' Marcus pulled a face.

'It was better than money. You could swap it for loads of things. Always dreamed of having my own salt mine.' Grampus got a faraway look in his eye.

As his mood seemed to have got better, I dared to ask him, 'Why have we never met Aunt Livia before?'

Grampus frowned. 'Rome is a long way away, you know.'

I sighed. 'I know, but did Mum ... do something bad?'

Grampus's eyes flashed. 'No! Your mother is a fine woman who has the misfortune of belonging to one of the leading families of Rome. She married my son against their wishes. They were forced to leave Rome. Your father joined the army where he earned his respect and honour instead of paying for it and we will do the same.'

'So Aunt Livia is rich, is she?' Marcus's ears pricked up. 'I think I shall like her.'

I groaned. My brother was such a predictable little toad!

There was a fine litter waiting outside the shop, carried by four of the hugest slaves I'd ever seen.

Livia climbed on saying, 'Hired them from the wrestling school. Now come along or we'll be late.'

Mum and I climbed on. As I fiddled with a velvet cushion I took one last look down the street to see if Philip had come back yet.

Marcus gave Aunt Livia a cheesy smile. 'You

do not need to go to a beauty parlour, Aunt Livia. You are beautiful enough.'

Livia beamed.

Then Marcus added, 'I've never seen anyone with two chins before.'

Mum quickly waved the men on as Aunt Livia said, 'Your children certainly have unusual manners. It must be because they have lived in Britain for too long. Nobody here knows how to behave properly. The sooner we get you properly married and back to Rome, the better.'

Mum did not say anything but she gripped tightly on to my arm until we arrived at the baths.

We were ushered into a private section that was much smarter than the usual bit of the baths that we go to. It was decorated in marble with fine mosaics. There were bowls of fruit, a woman strumming on a harp and the air stank of perfume. Lots of assistants glided around carrying mirrors, brushes and wearing cheesy grins. It was the last place on Earth I wanted to be.

'No one touches my eyebrows,' I hissed at an assistant who had shown me to a seat in front of a mirror.

'Suit yourself, dearie, but I'm under strict instructions to do something with that hair – then there's your nails, the Beer Froth face mask and the Dead Sea salt-scrub …'

She gave me a hard stare and a smug grin before she began piling my hair up on the top of my head and sticking pins in.

'Fine,' I grinned back. 'Oh, could you keep all the lice from my hair as I'm having a competition with Horace the Offal's dog?'

That wiped the smile off her face.

The whole business took ages. At the end of all that prodding and preening Aunt Livia didn't look much different, apart from the fact that she was now wearing an elaborate curly hairpiece and her cheeks were smudged.

Then Mum came out. Somehow they had wiped away the shadows from under her eyes.

She was wearing Egyptian eyeliner that reminded you how beautiful and brown her eyes were. Her nut brown hair had been curled and piled on top of her head, revealing how tall and elegant she was.

The four slaves carrying our litter cheered.

'Mum, what have they done? You look beautiful,' I gasped.

Mum replied, 'So would you, Drucilla, if you smiled.'

I snorted. Smile! I'd rather bite off the head of an asp! My head hurt with all my hair piled on top of it and I could only walk at a snail's pace in the long floaty dress they'd put on me. My gold earrings pinched and the sandals were tight.

After we had all climbed aboard, Aunt Livia said, 'There's someone I'd like you to meet. He's a high-ranking officer on a short visit from Rome. All he is in need of is a wife.'

'I'm not ready for marriage again,' Mum began, but Livia cut her off with a wave of her hand, saying, 'Nonsense. It's time you came back to Rome. With the right husband you could hold your head up high and maintain the family's honour. Please don't mention the fact that you work in a shop. It's so unladylike.'

The litter stopped at the entrance to the Forum where a soldier was standing.

'A man needs a woman,' Livia announced.

'Like a pot needs a crack in it,' I muttered under my breath. I didn't want Mum to get married again. The soldier turned round.

'And Pontius Maximus is such a fine man,' Livia said as the soldier came towards us.

My jaw opened and then froze in an 'O' shape like a startled fish.

Chapter Seven

I thought he was about to start complaining about his pots again. My face tensed up. Mum looked at her feet. Pontius made a big fuss of Aunt Livia and then he turned to us, bowed and spoke in an affected voice, 'So happy to make your acquaintance at last.'

The last time he saw Mum, she was dressed in her hessian work tunic and her hair was a mess. Now he kept looking at her with a googly-eyed expression and saying in an oily tone, 'Your great beauty is spoken of all the time in Rome. Indeed I have heard so much about you that I feel as if we have already met.'

I snorted and Mum pinched my arm.

Pontius and Aunt Livia were old friends who had travelled to Britain together. After a few minutes, Aunt Livia announced that she had to go and see the goldsmith about a new brooch for her cloak, so we were left alone in the street with Pontius.

He was all over Mum like a rash. How charmed he was to meet her, how much he'd heard about her great beauty in Rome, how brave she was to live in such a wild part of the Empire. It was truly stomach-churning stuff. No sign of the rude, brutish oaf who had bullied us in the shop or who had furiously hurled curses into the river.

Then he asked, 'I would be delighted if you and your charming family would do me the honour of attending a dinner party at my apartments in two days' time. I have commissioned an exquisite dinner service just for the occasion.'

'Was it very expensive?' I asked in a sweet voice.

Mum raised her eyebrow at me.

Pontius smiled. 'Let us just say money is no object when charm and beauty are to be honoured.'

'So you are going to pay a lot for it, then?' I persisted.

Mum jabbed me in the ribs. 'Forgive my daughter's rudeness. Thank you for your kind invitation but I don't think we can come.'

Aunt Livia chose that moment to come back. 'So, dinner is all arranged. Now we must be getting back.' She bustled us away.

As she dropped us off at the shop, she wrinkled her nose and said, 'The sooner we get you away from all this, the better!'

It was exactly the opposite of how I was feeling.

As soon as Marcus saw us, he demanded to have his hair set in curls too.

'Do you think Aunt Livia would like me more with curly hair?' he asked.

I offered to curl his tongue instead.

Grampus got all misty-eyed when he saw Mum. He sighed. 'You look as beautiful as the day you got married.'

'One of the reasons I got married was to escape Rome! I just wish I'd known how hard life was going to be!' Mum's eyes blazed. She made us get changed and set us to work finishing the dinner service that we were all going to eat off in two days time. Life is weird sometimes!

It was good to spend the rest of the day up to my arms in clay. Every time I twisted a piece of clay I thought about Pontius. I was slapping the clay about, imagining I was a beauty therapist working on Aunt Livia, when Philip came in carrying his collecting bag.

The curse! With all the business of the dinner invitation I had almost forgotten about it. By the look on his face he hadn't.

'Horace is a genius!' he said.

'I've heard him called some things before but never that. Next you'll be telling me he's invented his own perfume that all the women of the Empire desire.'

Philip looked at me sideways and asked, 'What's rattled your chariot?'

So I told him about meeting Pontius and the dinner invitation. I even told him what Aunt Livia had said about it being time for Mum to get married and go back to Rome.

'It would be terrible to be a rich girl in Rome. I wouldn't be allowed out of the house. I'd have to wear smart clothes all day. Then I'd be married off. Yuk!'

Philip patted my arm. 'Here's some good news. Horace has translated the curse.' He pulled it out from his bag. He began to laugh. 'It says, "A curse upon this pimple which will not leave my bottom."'

We spent a long time hugging ourselves with laughter about that.

'No wonder he's so grumpy most of the time.' I wiped a tear from my eye. 'I'd like nothing better than to send a plague on to his bottom. How about a plague of poisonous ants or flesh-eating beetles? Horace will know where we can get some.'

Philip shook his head. 'We have to help him get rid of the pimple that he was asking the gods to cure. Neptune or one of the other river gods would have sorted out the pimple and then a grateful Pontius would have left a big present.'

'So we have to sort the pimple so that Neptune gets his present?' I said.

'Gods are touchy about not getting presents. For revenge they could turn Marcus into an eel,' Phillip added.

A tempting thought – but Mum would be too upset.

Instead I said, 'How on Earth do you cure a bottom pimple?'

Philip sighed. 'I've no idea. I'm not a doctor.'

'But we know a man who is!' I grinned.

Philip shook his head. 'Dad never has any time to talk to me.'

I stood up. 'Then I shall go and see him.'

Chapter Eight

I didn't stop to wash the clay from my arms. I ran straight down the street and into Philip's house.

The small waiting room was packed with people when I barged in. I figured it would take at least two turns of the sand-timer before I got in to see Philip's dad. There wasn't even any space on a bench to sit down. How I wished I'd brought Horace with me. He'd have emptied the place in no time. I leaned against the doorframe, sighed heavily and rubbed my arms. Slivers of clay dropped off them. It gave me an idea.

'It's not all that infectious,' I said flippantly, as the woman nearest to me edged away. I continued, 'You should've seen the spots before they turned to scabs. They were terrible. My mum's thrown me out of the house, ever since the dog died of the same thing.'

And that was how I came to be the next person in line to see Philip's dad.

Philip's dad is tall, thin and extremely serious. Philip says he spends a lot of time thinking. I'm glad I don't think too much if it gives you such deep lines on your forehead.

He was standing by the window with his hands behind his back. 'Come over here, Drucilla, and stand next to me.'

I obeyed.

'Good. Now I want you to stick your tongue out as far it can go and pull the ugliest face that you can.'

Before I could open my mouth to protest he said, 'Go on, make the ugliest face you can.'

So I pulled my bug-eyed monster face.

'Good, very good.' He seemed pleased with the result.

'Am I healthy, then?' I asked.

'Who knows? I just can't stand the people

living opposite. Now, what's the matter with you?'

I squirmed a bit and hesitated.

He nodded knowingly and said, 'Let me guess, you've got a friend with an embarrassing problem.'

My eyes widened with amazement. How did he know that?

'This friend is having a terrible problem with a pimple that won't go away. It keeps coming back again.'

'Where exactly is this pimple?'

After a long pause I answered, 'In an embarrassing place.'

'Oh, I see.'

Philip's dad stroked his chin for a long time before saying, 'It's probably caused by an over-heating of the system. Cut down on the honey cakes. Jump in the coldest fridgidarium you can find and take a good purge. Pimples are unpleasant things. If that doesn't work there is another cure.'

'What's that?' I asked.

'It is a bit more drastic but some doctors speak of the "ass cure". The offending pimple is much improved by a sudden blow from the hind legs of an ass. This cure is not recommended for children unless they are extremely irritating.'

As he looked up at me, I noticed a little

twinkle in his eye. He thought I was talking about myself. I just had time for a double bluff.

'Thank you, I'll tell Marcus. Oops' – I covered my hand with my mouth – 'I promised not to tell!'

'Don't worry. It will be our little secret.' He tapped the side of his nose. 'Now, tell the next person to come in and run off home.'

I nodded and said as innocently as I could, 'I think I'm the last one.'

Outside I took some big gulps of fresh air. Doctors made me feel sick.

All that talk of honey cakes had made me hungry too. I was about to walk to the baker's when I noticed a group of soldiers surrounding the entrance to our shop.

Chapter Nine

There were four of them: one fat, one tall, one short, and a skinny one. The skinny one was standing in the doorway. He took a look at me and shouted, 'What's your business?'

I snarled back, 'What business is that of yours?'

He scratched his head.

The fat soldier joined him and said, 'The correct procedure, Quentin, is to take a step forward and say, "Halt, identify yourself!" whilst placing your sword thus.' He demonstrated a short jab with his own sword.

'Thanks, Sixtus. I can never remember.' He turned back to me, shouting, 'Halt yourself and identify.' He pulled out his sword and dropped it on his toe.

Sixtus tutted and the others sniggered.

Quentin coughed and tried again. 'Identify your halt and stop yourself, er—'

Sixtus rolled his eyes and said, 'Remember what happened to the first four soldiers that Pontius had in his bodyguard?'

Quentin's knees began to tremble.

I stood my ground. They weren't what you'd call a terrifying bunch.

The door of the shop opened and Marcus popped his head out. 'There you are. Mum is looking for you. Pontius has come to collect his pots. This is his bodyguard.'

'My mum wants me.' I looked at Quentin. 'Shall I tell her that you won't let me in? She gets very upset when people are mean to me. Did I tell you that she is the arm-wrestling champion of Londinium?'

Quentin looked flustered. He looked at one of the other soldiers. 'Sixtus, what does it say in the book about that?'

Sixtus looked blank and looked at the tall soldier. 'Septimus, what does it say in the book about that?'

Septimus scratched his head and said, 'Er I dunno, best ask Octavian.'

As Octavian was asleep upright against the wall they had to nudge him awake. Octavian blinked and smacked his lips and said, 'Let her in.'

I sighed and walked in. 'No wonder Rome wasn't built in a day.'

By contrast, it was a hive of activity in the shop. Even Marcus was busy packing some pots in straw.

Pontius leaned on the counter, polishing his fingernails whilst Grampus struggled with a heavy basket.

I tied a piece of hessian round my hair and rubbed some clay on my cheeks. Pontius kept on huffing and puffing like a tired horse. There was no sign of that sickly charm or a flicker of recognition. To him we were just servants and so beneath his notice.

Mum was looking hot and flustered. She snapped at me, 'Bring our guest some wine.'

Grampus made a harrumphing noise. There was only a little wine left and he liked to drink it 'to keep the cold out'.

As I handed the wine to Pontius I 'innocently' asked, 'Are you having some fine guests for dinner, then, sir?'

He looked down his nose at me before speaking in his sneery voice. 'I have fifty dormice being fattened in pots as we speak as well as a large tub of snails soaking in milk.'

I shuddered. We're not big fans of bloated snail or dormouse.

Pontius continued. 'My guests are used to the fine things in life. My dear friend, Livia, has a feast in her villa in Rome every week. Riches the likes of which you couldn't even begin to imagine. Her sister is the guest of honour. Her beauty and grace will tolerate only fine things.'

I glanced across at Mum. Her face was red from the heat of the kiln.

Marcus's voice piped up. 'I've got an Aunt Livia, too. You broke my toy chariot and you haven't offered to pay for a new one.'

I stamped on his foot behind the counter. 'Marcus loves his little jokes,' I added, smiling broadly.

Mum shot us a warning look and then cut in, 'Your dinner service is all packed and ready.'

Pontius opened the door and barked an order to the soldiers who trooped in and lined up. Skinny Quentin and small Octavian took a basket and fat Sixtus and tall Septimus took the other. The baskets hung lopsided.

Mum scratched up the final total on a wax tablet and handed Pontius the bill.

Pontius ordered the soldiers out of the shop, finished the glass of wine and then turned and said, 'Considering all the trouble you have put me through I will pay you after I have held the dinner party.'

After he had gone, Mum slumped down on a pile of straw and wiped a tear from her eye. Marcus and I sat down beside her.

I squeezed her hand and said, 'It'll be all right, Mum. People will always need pots!'

'But will they always pay for them? I can't go on like this. I have to pay the rent. It's not fair on you. I think I'm going to have to follow Livia's advice: go to the party and take you all back to Rome. At least you'll all be treated with respect there.'

My stomach lurched. Mum was going to marry Pontius!

I ran out of the shop and slumped down on a stone bench in the street.

Chapter Ten

If only Aunt Livia hadn't come stirring things up, we would have carried on as we were. That was our curse – meeting up with her and her fancy Roman ways.

I felt so frustrated that I did something I hate: I let a couple of tears slide down my face. I only do that when I'm alone. Suddenly I felt a bony finger on my hand which made me jump. It was Sybil!

'Why the waterworks, Drucilla?' she asked.

I rubbed my face. 'That wasn't a tear. My eyes were too hot. It was sweat.'

Sybil sat down next to me and gently patted my leg.

'I have exactly the same problem. My eyes sweat terribly in the summer or when I'm worried. Is there something on your mind?'

So I told her all about Pontius, the curse and going back to Rome. I got it all off my chest. Sybil didn't say very much, she just listened.

'What's it like in Rome?' I asked her.

Sybil screwed up her eyes and thought about

it for a while.

'The Rome that I can see is full of bright lights without fire, chariots pulled by a power other than horses. The people are wearing strange dark shades over their eyes and licking frozen cow's milk. I can just about see the Coliseum but it is all in ruins.'

'Do you like seeing into the future all the time?' I asked.

'Sometimes I wish I wasn't so long-sighted. My friend, Oona, can only see up to three weeks into the future. That makes her a big hit at parties and with senators and gamblers. I'll take you to see her some time. She wears the most fabulous costumes. People really listen to what she has to say ...' Her voice trailed off and she looked really sad.

'But you are much better than Oona. You can see so far into the future that it doesn't hurt anyone.'

We smiled at each other.

Sybil wiped the sweat from my eyes and said, 'I think between us we can come up with a way out of this mess.'

* * *

There was only Grampus in the shop when I got back. He was furiously sweeping the floor and muttering. Bits of straw clung to the wisps of his hair.

'I don't know who that Pontius thinks he is. In my day you showed respect to your elders.'

Time to start putting Sybil's plan into action!

I smiled and said, 'Look on the bright side, Grampus. There's bound to be some good food and wine to eat off our plates at this party. You can put your army uniform on.'

Grampus's eyes lit up and he wet his lips. 'If he's brought some olives and anchovy paste with him, that would go down nicely with some wine.' Then he gripped hard on to the handle of the brush and shook his head. 'He'll recognise us from the shop. Your mother will be disgraced. We can't go!'

He had a point. A scrubbed-up Mum and me could just about pull it off but not if you added Marcus and Grampus. No amount of scrubbing up could alter Grampus. As for Marcus, he would have to wear a bag over his head to be unrecognisable. Trouble was, I needed to get to the party and for us not to be recognised by Pontius.

As if on cue, Marcus came in munching on a bowl of blackberries. 'What's the problem? You look like you've just had a visit from the tax collector. Is Mum not back from meeting Aunt Livia yet? She's been gone ages.'

'As soon as we enter Pontius's apartments he'll put two and two together and recognise us from the shop,' I explained.

Grampus scratched his head. 'There may be a way. A little military cunning may be required. Remember the Greeks hid in that wooden horse to sneak into Troy?'

'I'm not spending the evening hiding in a wooden crate!' Marcus groaned.

'He means we could alter our appearance,' I sighed.

Marcus frowned at me. 'It might work. They made you look pretty, after all.'

'Curl up and dye!' Grampus said and banged the counter.

'No way am I going to give in,' I snapped back.

Grampus laughed. 'Neither are we. I mean that Marcus and I are going to curl up and dye our hair. Horace has promised me some false teeth to fill in the gaps. In the army I was a master of disguise.'

* * *

'I'll put on the tunic that Aunt Livia bought me and put my hair up,' I said, pinching a berry from Marcus's bowl and popping it into my mouth as Philip came in.

'Weird patient came running in to see Father today. He burst in the room shouting, "I'm gladiator! I'm gladiator!" Dad made him sit down and have a drink of water. "Don't you mean to say I am a gladiator?" my dad replied. He hates sloppy language. The man looked perplexed, "But I'm not a gladiator. I'm glad he ate her!" It turned out that his pet crocodile had eaten his annoying next-door neighbour and he was pleased about it.'

I handed him the bowl of berries. 'For that you can give us a hand mixing up some hair dye before Mum comes back.'

Chapter Eleven

Philip did his best but Grampus and Marcus both looked like they'd had a fight with the bowl of blackberries and the berries had won.

'It's taken years off me,' Grampus laughed.

'Which ones?' Marcus asked.

Half of one side of Grampus's face was now tinged deep purple. He had definitely shrunk since the days he was a soldier. His uniform now hung on him at least two sizes too big.

'And how are you going to alter your appearance, Drucilla?' Philip asked as he wiped the dye off his hands.

'Don't worry about me. I'll just brush my hair and smile,' I said.

Philip's cheeks flushed as he said in a quiet voice, 'I like you just the way you are.'

Now it was my turn to go berry red.

Before I could say or do anything Horace, Sybil and Cano walked in.

'Brought you some false teeth. Made them myself.' Horace put a parcel down on the counter.

Cano whined.

Horace patted his head. 'Don't worry, I'll get you another bone.'

Sybil was staring at Grampus and Marcus with 'that look' in her eye.

'In the future people will dye their hair strange colours and play on loud musical instruments. They will wear chains, shackles and dog collars. They are called punk rockers.'

'Grampus, we could be skunk rockers,' Marcus yelled.

Grampus shook his head. 'No one puts a dog collar on me!'

'But you'll happily put a dog's bone in your mouth.' I rolled my eyes.

Horace held one up. 'They're hand-carved to look like teeth.'

'You could go into business. I'm sure lots of people need replacement teeth,' Philip suggested.

Horace shook his head. 'Sybil says there's no future in it. At least not for the next five hundred years.'

'I know one thing for sure,' Sybil said. 'Your mother is looking very beautiful.'

Sybil was right. Mum had appeared in the doorway in her new dress. She smiled sadly and said, 'We all look splendid but ... Oh dear, I should never have let Livia talk me into it. We can't go!' She kept shaking her head and twisting her hands. I groaned. When Mum makes up her mind, there is no changing it. I had to get to the party!

Grampus sighed. 'I was so looking forward to eating some calves' brain custard.'

Marcus whined, 'And I was going to win Aunt Livia's undying affection so that she'll grant my every wish.'

I stuck my chin out. 'I've gone to a lot of trouble to prepare for tonight.' If she only knew how much!

Mum began taking off the bangles on her arms and said, 'I'm going to get changed. There's plenty of work to be getting on with.'

Horace screwed up his nose. 'Eeugh! What's that stink?'

Cano howled as Aunt Livia wafted in, followed by an overpowering smell of rose petals and spices.

Horace fled from the shop, holding his nose and saying, 'How can the rest of you bear that stink?'

Sybil rushed after him, only stopping to give me a wink.

Even if Aunt Livia's face hadn't been caked in white make-up it would have cracked at the sight of us. She wrinkled her nose, looked at each one of us carefully and said in a haughty voice, 'Is this really the best you can do?'

She rearranged Mum's hair and sighed. 'Thank goodness we're not in Rome. The Britons have no taste or style so we might just get away with it.'

Mum's eyes flashed. She put back on all the bangles, turned to Aunt Livia and said, 'My family is good enough to be seen anywhere. You can stay here if you'd rather not be seen with us.'

And so we set off.

* * *

Pontius was back in an oily mood as he ushered us into his apartment. It was filled with fancy couches, laden with fine silk cushions. A beautiful fountain filled with petals was in the middle of the room. Everything glittered with newness from the marble floor to the group of musicians.

I wonder if he's paid for all of this yet? I asked myself as I gazed around the room.

Marcus and I were shunted to the bottom end of the room and given two uncomfortable chairs to sit on. We were also right next to the lyre player who was struggling to get the notes

in the right order for the tune.

'This isn't fair. Aunt Livia promised that I could sit next to her and share her food,' Marcus complained. 'I think I'm going to like living like this in Rome.'

'With a bully like that as a stepfather?'

'I'll be spending most of my time at Aunt Livia's.'

'You'll be spending most of your time at school. And then, for your military training – ice-cold baths and hand-to-hand combat from morning until night. That will soon toughen you up.'

I think I went a bit too far because Marcus went pale and suddenly lost his appetite.

'Don't worry, Marcus, I have a plan.'

Time for me to spring into action!

I sneaked out during the rather wobbly display of military positions that Pontius's bodyguard was putting on for our entertainment. Quentin nearly poked Septimus in the eyes whilst attempting to execute the 'Tortoise'. Marcus didn't help matters by firing olive stones at their ankles.

I edged slowly towards the kitchens where I hoped Sybil would be waiting for me.

Chapter Twelve
Marcus Takes Over ...

Drucilla asked me to take over the telling of the next bit of the story. About time too! That girl witters on far too much. I may be younger but I am heaps smarter than her. I found the curse, didn't I? Wasn't it my toy chariot that Pontius fell over in the first place? Let's face it – there would be nothing to tell if it wasn't for me.

I was in a foul mood. This party was not going as I expected. I should have been at the top table snuggling up to Aunt Livia. She likes me and it would suit me fine being rich. I'm very good at lounging around on couches eating sweet things. I would be very kind to all my servants. They could have one day off each year. Instead, I had to sit on a wobbly stool next to the world's worst lyre player and listen to my sweet sister's acid predictions about what my life would really be like in Rome. There's no way I'm going into the army.

Speaking of which, after the terrible music, Pontius's bodyguards tried to put on a display of military might. They demonstrated a military manoeuvre called the 'Tortoise'. They arranged their shields over their heads into a shape that is supposed to strike terror into the enemy. I suppose you can die laughing. I showed my appreciation by aiming olive stones at their ankles and making the 'Tortoise' wobble. At some point during this display Drucilla disappeared.

A group of dancing girls came on after that. They were a slight improvement on Pontius's bodyguard. One of them dragged me up to dance with her.

It was really hard wobbling your tummy and moving your arms in different directions but after a while I got the hang of it and was swirling around the room. It was hot work and I forgot about the hair dye that splattered a few of the dinner guests.

I flopped down on a cushion near to Grampus. He was too busy filling his face and boring anyone who would listen with his army tales. I was trying hard to catch Aunt Livia's eye when a clatter of a tambourine made everyone freeze in mid-air and Oona the Soothsayer was introduced.

Another loud bang of the tambourine and this weird-looking creature, dressed from head to foot in brightly-coloured scarves, came into the room.

Pontius sat up and looked cross. 'I didn't order a soothsayer. Where's the dancing bear?'

Oona rattled her tambourine and spoke in a wavy voice. 'The dancing bear has developed two left paws and so I have been sent to entertain you instead.'

Pontius pursed his lips and said, 'Very well.'

Oona banged her tambourine again (this was getting pretty boring and I was about to reach for the olive stones). As she raised her arm, there was a loud bang followed by a puff of smoke. That got everyone's attention.

Oona began swaying and rolling her eyes. Then she opened her eyes really wide and said, 'I see a man in a uniform. Is there someone in this room called Quentin?'

One of the soldiers waved his arm.

Oona did not look at him but continued speaking. 'You are not following your heart's desire. Leave your job and do what you really want.'

Quentin jumped up. 'For years I dreamed of growing apples and then distilling the juice into a drink.' He ran out of the door.

The tambourine banged again.

'I have a message for someone very important in this room. His name begins with a …' Oona screwed up her eyes. 'A "B" – no this person's name begins with a letter "P". This person has recently dropped a curse into the river.'

Pontius dropped a plate on to the floor. Then he muttered, 'Any fool can find out the name of the owner of this apartment.'

'I can clearly see what is written upon it. The words of the curse say, "A plague on this pim—"'

Pontius roared, 'Enough of this, soothsayer! Haven't you got anything more entertaining than this to tell us?'

'But I can help this person with the pim—'

Pontius interrupted again. 'Get on with it,

then. Tell us how you can help this person with the pimple.'

Everyone roared laughing at the word pimple.

Oona continued. 'It's very simple. All that "P" has to do is pay double for any new objects that he has recently bought, like spoons or a … perhaps even a dinner service. This will impress the gods with his generosity. Then "P" should return to Rome as speedily as possible and not consider marrying for at least another ten years, or he'll end up with hundreds of pimples, warts and assorted scabs all over his big fat—'

Mum stood up at this point and said, 'Enough of this, Soothsayer. Do not push your luck too far.' Which I thought was a weird comment to make.

Oona rattled her tambourine, twizzled her scarves and left the room.

Drucilla came back from the Vomitorium or wherever she had sloped off to. As we were getting our cloaks on to go home I whispered, 'You missed the soothsayer. She was fantastic. She knew all about the curse. I had loads of things that I wanted to ask her.'

'Like what, exactly?'

I sighed. 'There's no point wasting my breath telling you.'

Drucilla collapsed in a heap of giggles.

I'd always suspected my sister was mad as well as grumpy – now I knew it for sure.

Chapter Thirteen
Back to Drucilla ...

'A funny thing happened in the forum yesterday. Pontius and what was left of his bodyguard were on their way to pay the mosaic-maker double what they owed him when a boy and his donkey blocked their path.

'"Move your ass!" Pontius shouted. He obviously wasn't enjoying being parted from his money. The boy, who was extremely polite and sensible-looking, went to pat the donkey. Sadly, he must've pricked the donkey by accident because it jumped up and landed a hoof on Pontius's pimple. Before Pontius could compose himself, the boy and the donkey had melted into the crowd.'

We all laughed when Philip told us this story.

'Well, I thought it was only fair to administer the correct cure,' he said.

Mum handed him another honey cake and winked at me. 'I think "Oona" did that, didn't she, Drucilla?'

Grampus giggled and tapped his nose.

'She did it doubly!' Pontius had paid Mum

twice the agreed amount.

'I'm surprised that Oona couldn't see that I was never going to marry such an oaf as Pontius.'

'You weren't?' I asked.

Sybil and Horace came into the shop carrying a large wicker basket.

Sybil smiled. 'We picked this up very cheap at a certain soldier's leaving sale. Thought you might be able to sell them again.'

Horace opened up the basket and there was a familiar-looking red dinner service.

We all groaned.

'They're all in perfect condition. There are no cracks in them.' Horace looked pleased.

We all groaned again.

'You can keep those pots!' I laughed.

As they were leaving, Sybil looked up at me. 'One day, Drucilla, you are going to grow up into a fine young woman.'

'Are we going back to Rome, then?' Marcus looked up from playing with his new toy chariot.

Mum shook her head. 'I think we're all happier here in Londinium for the moment.'

Marcus stuck out his bottom lip.

Mum patted him on the head. 'Never mind. Philip's father has sent you a delicious tonic drink. He dropped it in this morning. He said you had Drucilla to thank for it.'

I'd forgotten about my double bluff story at the doctor's. How could I explain that I'd pretended it was Marcus who had the pimple?

'I wouldn't drink that if I were you, Marcus,' I warned.

Marcus looked at me. 'You're just jealous because people like me more than you and want to give me presents.'

'You're so right, Marcus. You really deserve that drink,' I replied and watched him drink it down in three big gulps.

Then Mum turned to me. 'Do try and stay out of trouble, Drucilla.'

What had I done?

Look out for more

fantastic fiction in

Black Cats ...

TERRY DEARY
Footsteps in the Fog

Laura Lund's family is rich.
Tommy Pickford's family is poor,
but he and Laura are best friends
and look out for each other all the time.

Their school, Meek Street Primary,
is having a special mid-winter treat:
a show starring the famous magician,
The Great Marvello.

But Marvello's tricks seem too good
to be true, and soon Tommy and
Laura are plunged into danger …

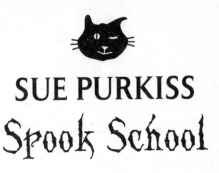

SUE PURKISS
Spook School

What could be worse for a ghost
than not being spooky enough?

That's Spooker's problem as he faces his
all-important Practical Haunting exam.
It doesn't help that his task is to haunt
a brand new house – hardly the kind
of dark, dingy place where ghosts
are meant to dwell!

But when Spooker makes a new
friend, he might just find a solution
to his problems.

PHILIP WOODERSON
Moonmallow Smoothie

Sam's dad runs an ice cream parlour,
but his business is fast melting
away, thanks to competition from
Karbunkle's Mega Emporiums.

Then, suddenly one night,
a meteorite crashes to Earth in Sam's
garden. It's not just space-rock –
its special properties are perfect for
making ice cream. Soon everyone
wants a taste of Dad's latest invention,
called Moonmallow Smoothie.

But Sam's troubles are only
just beginning …

GEORGIA BYNG
The Ramsbottom Rumble

'If that Arthur is for real, I'll eat my ...'
'Baseball cap?' suggested Dan.
'My skateboard,' said Tom.

Arthur Ramsbottom is Gran's boyfriend,
and he claims to work for the Secret
Service. Tom and Dan are pretty sure
he's up to no good, but it's going to
take all their acting skills if they are
to catch him ...

KAREN WALLACE
Something Slimy on Primrose Drive

When Pearl Wolfbane and her family
move into No. 34 Primrose Drive,
everything soon becomes murky, weird
and crumbling. Except for Pearl's room.
It stays pink, frilly and normal because
Pearl isn't like the rest of her family.

When Pearl meets her neighbours,
the Rigid-Smythes, she is delighted.
They have a swimming pool, not a
swamp; a kitchen, not a dungeon.

But they also have a daughter
called Ruby, and she isn't like her
family either …

Other titles available in Black Cats ...

Great stories for hungry readers